A Mother's Journey

Sarthak Kathuria

BlueRose ONE
Stories Matter
New Delhi • London

BLUEROSE PUBLISHERS
India | U.K.

BlueRose ONE
Stories Matter
New Delhi • London

For permissions requests or inquiries regarding this publication,
please contact:

BLUEROSE PUBLISHERS
www.BlueRoseONE.com
info@bluerosepublishers.com
+91 8882 898 898
+4407342408967

ISBN: 978-93-7139-021-7

Cover Design: Aman Sharma
Typesetting: Pooja Sharma

First Edition: May 2025

A Mother's **Journey**

Table of Contents

Chapter 1: Bound by Tradition

A woman from West Delhi married a man from the same area, chosen by her father. Before their wedding, they met a few times. During one meeting, the man touched her shoulder. Unsettled by the gesture, she confided in her parents, expressing her discomfort. However, they dismissed her concerns, saying, "We cannot judge him based on this alone." The wedding went ahead as planned.

The man had two sisters. One of whom lived in the same house with them after her marriage fell apart. She stayed there with her daughter. The woman worked at a pharmaceutical company, while her husband was a salesman at a shoe store. In the beginning, the marriage appeared to be going well. They even went on a honeymoon—though not alone. The husband's sisters and their children accompanied them, making it more of a family trip than an intimate getaway.

Over time, the man became increasingly fixated on having a son. He would often say to his wife, "I only want a boy in the family." His other sister, though living elsewhere, often visited their home. Her husband was a compulsive gambler, regularly betting on cricket matches. Because of their financial struggles, they were renting a small place in West Delhi.

Thus began the woman's journey into marriage—a life shaped by family expectations, unspoken struggles, and dreams yet to unfold.

Chapter 2: A Prayer and a New Beginning

Time moved swiftly. They married in 1998, and in 1999, a son was born in ESI Hospital in West Delhi. During her stay in the maternity ward, my mother found herself alone—no family member had come to bring her food. Hungry and exhausted, she turned to the other women in the ward, asking if anyone had leftovers to spare. With kindness, they shared a meal with her, easing her hunger.

Not long after, one of her sisters-in-law arrived with food, but by then, she had already eaten. As she lay waiting to go into labor, she prayed fervently for a son. In India, it was impossible to know the baby's gender before birth, leaving the answer to fate.

Then the moment arrived—a son was born into the family. At that time, he was the only boy among the children, as the two sisters-in-law had daughters. One of them lived in the same household, making his birth feel even more significant—a rare occurrence in the family, a moment that would be remembered for years.

His arrival marked more than just the birth of a child, it was the beginning of a new chapter for everyone—one shaped by tradition, hope, and an unspoken wish finally fulfilled.

Chapter 3: Bound by Tradition, Trapped by Circumstance

The mother's relationship with her in-laws was far from healthy. Coming from a modest-income family, she carried the burden of financial struggles, worsened by the fact that her parents had borrowed money from her husband and were unable to repay it on time. This debt became a source of constant humiliation for her, as her mother-in-law frequently yelled at her, demanding that she retrieve the money from her parents. At times, she was even thrown out of the house.

Whenever she tried to leave, she pleaded to take her young son with her, but her in-laws refused, making it impossible for her to escape the toxic environment. Knowing they would never let her take her child, she felt utterly trapped. Her in-laws were wealthier than her own family; they owned their house, while her parents lived in a rented home. She knew that no matter where she turned, she had nowhere to go.

When she returned to her parents' home, instead of being offered refuge, she was urged to go back to her husband's house. Her father, desperate to keep peace and avoid the shame of his daughter's failing marriage, would bring her back to her in-laws and plead with them to accept her again. At the time, divorce was rare, especially among lower middle class families in India, which made her options severely limited. Left with no choice, she had to return to the same home where she was disrespected and mistreated.

This chapter of her life was filled with silent suffering, societal expectations, and an unbreakable cycle that kept her bound to an oppressive reality. Yet deep within her, a quiet resilience was building, quietly preparing for a day when she could finally reclaim her voice.

Chapter 4: A Year of Resilience

As time waits for none, days passed swiftly, bringing her son's first birthday closer. With both parents working full-time, the little boy was often cared for by his grandfather and mother, and occasionally by his maternal grandmother. Wanting to make the day special, his mother invited her colleagues and family to join the celebration, including her husband's paternal family, who were expected to be present. The gathering was simple—nothing extravagant, just a warm and meaningful celebration fitting for a middle class family. Yet, it was filled with joy, laughter, and heartfelt wishes.

But soon, an unexpected tragedy struck. Her husband, overwhelmed by unresolved tensions with his mother—fuelled by misunderstandings caused by his sister-in-law—set himself on fire. The severity of his injuries led to his immediate admission to a Delhi hospital. Thankfully, given her experience in the pharmaceutical industry, she leveraged her professional connections to ensure that he received the best possible care. Through these efforts, he was stabilized, and his life was saved.

Every morning, before heading to work, she visited the hospital, ensuring he felt supported through the recovery process. While some family members, including his younger sister, hesitated to enter the 'burn' ward, she remained steadfast, determined to see him through this ordeal. The recovery was arduous, stretching over a year, during which she became the family's sole breadwinner, shouldering the financial burden while keeping the household afloat.

Through resilience and sheer will, she carried her family forward. But the scars—both seen and unseen—were yet to fully heal.

What lies ahead? Will time mend the wounds, or will new trials emerge?

Chapter 5: Shadows of Resilience: A Mother's Silent Struggle

Despite the challenges, the mother continued working at the same company, receiving support from her workplace during tough times. However, her sisters-in-law often visited her home, provoking conflict with her mother-in-law. This led to her being treated disrespectfully when she returned from work. Her partner occasionally supported her, but the situation remained tense.

At this time, one of the sisters-in-law lived with them, while the other visited frequently, causing further discord. Amidst the chaos, her child was growing quickly and had started school, where he was learning and thriving. She would return home each day to help her son with his schoolwork, nurturing his growth despite the challenges.

The grandmother, however, seemed more focused on her daughter's child, prioritising her over her grandson. The two sisters-in-law often used inappropriate language, calling both the mother and son names and suggesting that they didn't belong in the house. While the rest of the family supported her, her husband's support was inconsistent. As a mother, she felt deeply hurt but knew she couldn't leave the house, fearing she wouldn't be able to take her son with her.

Will she find the strength to reclaim her dignity and protect her son, or will the shadows of her circumstances continue to loom over her? The journey unfolds.

Chapter 6: The Final Breath

Time waits for no one—her mother-in-law often reminded her of this harsh truth, emphasizing that nothing would be given to her or her child from the family's possessions. As a mother, she worked tirelessly every day to provide for the family's needs, while her son—who was about to start second grade—was cared for by his grandfather, who picked him up from school every afternoon.

Her mother-in-law, an asthma patient, had been prescribed daily medication to maintain her health. However, one fateful day, she began feeling unwell. When her daughter-in-law returned home, she immediately decided to take her to the place they had always gone for medical emergencies. But before they could even reach the doctor, her mother-in-law took her final breath, succumbing to what appeared to be a heart attack.

Despite the devastating realization, she still took her to the doctor, hoping that something could be done. But the diagnosis was final—the elderly woman had passed away. In shock and sorrow, she returned home and informed the family, bearing the weight of the painful news.

The grief was overwhelming, yet the family gathered together and followed all the sacred rituals prescribed by the *Arya Samaj* tradition. In the face of loss, they found solace in unity, honouring the life of their beloved matriarch in the only way they knew—through remembrance, tradition, and love.

Chapter 7: Tangled Ties and Silent Battles

The journey began once more, with six people now sharing the same household. Among them were a sister-in-law with her daughter, she herself, her husband, her father-in-law, and her son. Life under the same roof was never simple, especially when an unseen wedge drove relationships apart.

Her husband's younger sister frequently visited their home, but instead of bringing warmth, she carried whispers. She filled her father's ears with resentment, turning him against his son and daughter-in-law. Previously, the mother-in-law had been the one to stir conflict, but now, it was the father-in-law who ensured their happiness remained out of reach. Neither of the sisters led a fulfilled life—one's marriage had already crumbled, and the other was bond by shackles through her marriage to a gambler. Her husband squandered his earnings betting on matches, amassing debts he could never repay.

In a bid to offer them stability, her father-in-law urged his son to help. Dutifully, he bought them a house in their name, believing he was giving them a fresh start. Yet, the change he had expected never came. The younger sister's husband remained addicted to gambling, eventually pawning the house papers for loans, sinking deeper into financial ruin. Desperate, he sought guidance from an Indian *guru*, who told him that the mother and son would waste their wealth and bring disaster.

Destiny followed no prophecy, and their lives unfolded in ways unforeseen.

One day, the father-in-law sent his son to the younger sister's house, claiming that his daughter had been hurt. That night, she returned home in tears, seeking refuge. Coincidentally, the other sister-in-law had just moved out to live with her husband. Though the number of people remained six, the household dynamics had shifted once again—with the younger sister-in-law and her child now becoming part of the house.

Their tangled lives continued; bound by duty yet fractured by distrust, each struggling to find happiness in a home where peace was always fleeting.

Chapter 8: Shackled by Silence

She had always known her family was far from perfect, but the truth of her distorted reality became undeniable now. For some time, her younger sister-in-law stayed with her, offering an illusion of companionship. Yet, the house—legally in her name—remained a hollow refuge. Her husband, absent at times, was no relief. When he was present, his anger filled every corner like a relentless storm.

He was a man who demanded obedience. His temper ruled their home, and his fists punctuated his frustration. If something displeased him—if the food wasn't to his taste, if she had forgotten a minor instruction—she bore the consequences. The yelling, the slaps, the threats became routine, woven into the very fabric of their marriage. From the very beginning, love had never been part of their union. She was merely a source of income, a decision imposed upon him by his father.

In the tradition of arranged marriages still prevalent in parts of India, they had never even met before the wedding. There had been no courtship, no choice—only duty and expectation. She was trapped, the weight of her circumstances pressing against her. How long could she endure this silence?

Would she ever break free?

Chapter 9: Echoes of Solitude: A Chapter of Loss, Lockdown, and Unexpected Conversations

The world had shifted. Her son had successfully finished school and was preparing to go abroad for further studies. Meanwhile, life at home had changed in ways no one could have anticipated. Her sister-in-law no longer lived with them, but grief still lingered in the walls of their home, as her father-in-law had passed away the previous year after a long battle with blood cancer. She had been his pillar of strength, caring for him through the arduous three years of his illness.

Then, the pandemic struck. Cities emptied, workplaces shut down, and people withdrew into their homes. She and her husband were suddenly alone in their house, where silence settled in like an unwelcomed guest. The streets were deserted, yet neighbours would occasionally come by to play cards or indulge in small games—tiny attempts to make time feel less oppressive. With everyone confined indoors, work had paused for many. Some essential workers were summoned back to duty, but she and her husband remained at home.

Working remotely became her new reality. She coordinated tasks, passed on instructions, and kept things moving, often communicating with her fellow employees. One of them—a younger colleague—had become a frequent voice in her day-to-day interactions. He shared snippets of his life, speaking of his girlfriend, his joys, his uncertainties. She listened, offering responses, advice, and an ear to his musings.

Day after day, their exchanges continued. Conversations blurred the boundaries between professional and personal, and amidst the lingering quiet of lockdown, human connection found its own way to persist.

Little did she know that in these moments of shared thoughts, the course of her days—and perhaps even her life—was beginning to shift in ways she never expected.

Chapter 10: Shattered Trust

She never imagined that her life would take such a turn. At first, it was just subtle suspicion—her husband's lingering glances at her phone, the quiet tension in the air whenever she messaged a colleague. But soon, his doubts grew into something darker.

While working from home, she often had professional conversations with a coworker, a man who confided in her about his struggles with his relationship. She offered him wisdom from her own experiences, explaining how women think, hoping to help him understand. But knowing her husband's possessive nature, she deleted their conversations, not out of guilt, but because she feared his reaction.

Suspicion turned into obsession. Her husband started monitoring her texts, checking her phone at every opportunity. One day, he decided to test her loyalty. He messaged her coworker from her phone, pretending to be her. The response was innocuous—a simple "Did you wake up so early?" But when an unexpected link arrived in return, curiosity consumed him. Transferring the link to his own phone, he was met with content that sent him into a violent rage.

Blinded by fury, he grabbed a wooden rod and lashed out. The blows rained down, each one a twisted manifestation of his distrust. In that moment, fear outweighed pain. Without hesitation, she fled—no phone, no belongings—only desperation guiding her steps. She sought refuge in a relative's home in another city, longing to reunite with her child, who was abroad.

Meanwhile, her husband, unable to find her, reported her disappearance to the police with his brother-in-law by his side. Time passed, but the scars remained. When she finally gathered the courage to call her son, she recounted everything—every betrayal, every bruise, every ounce of fear. It shattered her son. In anguish, he confronted his father, demanding him to bring her back. But even then, her voice trembled whenever they spoke—because no matter the distance, she knew what kind of man her husband was. He was a storm that never learned to calm.

Chapter 11: A Fragile Return

She never imagined that her life would take such a turn. At first, it was just subtle suspicion—her husband's lingering glances at her phone, the quiet tension in the air whenever she messaged a colleague. But soon, his doubts grew into something darker.

While working from home, she often had professional conversations with a coworker, a man who confided in her about his struggles with his relationship. She offered him wisdom from her own experiences, explaining how women think, hoping to help him understand. But knowing her husband's possessive nature, she deleted their conversations, not out of guilt, but because she feared his reaction.

Suspicion turned to obsession. Her husband started monitoring her texts, checking her phone at every opportunity. One day, he decided to test her loyalty. He messaged her coworker from her phone, pretending to be her. The response was innocuous—a simple "Did you wake up so early?" But when an unexpected link arrived in return, curiosity consumed him. Transferring the link to his own phone, he was met with content that sent him into a violent rage.

Blinded by fury, he grabbed a wooden rod and lashed out. The blows rained down, each one a twisted manifestation of his distrust. In that moment, fear outweighed pain. Without hesitation, she fled—no phone, no belongings—only desperation guiding her steps. She sought refuge in a relative's home in another city, longing to reunite with her child, who was abroad.

Meanwhile, her husband, unable to find her, reported her disappearance to the police with his brother-in-law by his side. Time passed, but the scars remained. When she finally gathered the courage to call her child, she recounted everything—every betrayal, every bruise, every ounce of fear. It shattered her son. In anguish, he confronted his father, demanding he bring her back. But even then, her voice trembled whenever they spoke—because no matter the distance, she knew what kind of man her husband was. He was a storm that never learned to calm.

Chapter 12: The Final Sacrifice

In a world brimming with mysteries, what had transpired remained shrouded in secrecy. She lived in her PG, visiting her husband's place on weekends. Yet, a strange unease lingered—someone was watching her, tracking her every move. Was it mere paranoia, or had they truly hired someone to spy on her? She had done nothing wrong, yet the shadows clung to her like an omen.

Her in-laws orchestrated a sinister plot, recording videos and blackmailing her into creating an account under the name of "Nikki Rani." Their intent was clear—to strip her of dignity, to brand her as someone without character in society. Her son, thousands of miles away, remained oblivious to the horrors unfolding back home. In his absence, they ensured she lived in perpetual fear, unable to reclaim control over her own life.

But this was more than mere intimidation. It was manslaughter—not in the physical sense, but the murder of her soul, her identity, her very existence. They manipulated her into actions that would tarnish her reputation, ensuring she was defamed beyond redemption. Her sister-in-law's husband—a gambler—had a *guru* who orchestrated everything, weaving ancient chants and "*jaadu tona*" into the fabric of their scheme. A curse was cast, an illusion spun, making her bend to their will.

Yet, despite their machinations, she stood unbroken. Every torment, every humiliation, every sacrifice—she endured it all for one reason: her son. She longed for the day he would return after three long years, hoping that by then, the storm would have passed. The scars would remain, but she refused to let them define her.

As she gazed into the horizon, waiting for the day of reunion, she whispered to herself:

"They tried to bury me, but they didn't know I was a seed."